MY BOOK OF
STUPID JOKES

this boOk belongs to:

Based on the TV series *Angela Anaconda*®
created by Joanna Ferrone and Sue Rose as seen on the Fox Family Channel®

SIMON SPOTLIGHT
An imprint of Simon & Schuster Children's Publishing Division
1230 Avenue of the Americas, New York, New York 10020

Manufactured in the United States of America

First Edition
10 9 8 7 6 5 4 3 2 1

ISBN 0-689-83994-4

{family}

Angela Anaconda™

MY BOOK OF STUPID JOKES

**written by
David Lewman**

Simon Spotlight

New York   London   Toronto   Sydney   Singapore

Ninnie Poo

Angela: If I lie out in the sun, who do I become?

Gina: Tangela Tanaconda.

Angela: Which kind of net stinks the worst?

Gordy: A fishing net?

Angela: No, a Nanette!

Angela: What do you get when you cross Ninnie Poo with a salamander?

Gina: Nanewt Manoir!

Angela: Where does Nanette Man-Wart sleep at night?
Gina: In a Nan-nest!

Angela: Why did the squirrel grab Nanette Manoir?
Gina: He thought she was a Nan-nut!

Angela: If you squished Nin Poo in her own diary, who would she become?
Gina: Nanette Memoir.

Gordy: What's the worst part about Tapwater Springs?

Angela: It's got lots of drips.

Gordy: Why doesn't Gina mind when Nanette teases her?

Angela: On account of Gina always has the Lash laugh.

Johnny: What did Angela do when her best friend got trapped in a jar?

Gordy: She let the Gina out of the bottle.

8

Which of Angela's friends is part pumpkin?
Gourdy Rhinehart.

Johnny: Who wears glasses, wheezes, and loves to hang around in museums?
Gina: Gordy Fineart!

How is Gina like Gordy's medicine when she eats?
They're both inhalers.

12

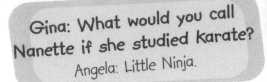

Gina: What would you call Nanette if she studied karate?
Angela: Little Ninja.

How is Angela's teacher like a pen?
In "Mrs. Brinks," you'll find "ink."

Gen: Why did Nanette act nice to Baby Lulu?
Bill: She wanted to be the teether's pet.

Gordy: Why did Nanette keep bugging Mrs. Brinks?

Angela: On account of she wanted to be the teacher's pest.

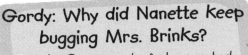

Why does Angela try to find out if Mrs. Brinks is a nudist?

She wants to know the naked truth.

Gina: When is Mrs. Brinks like an uncooked carrot?

Angela: When she's in the raw.

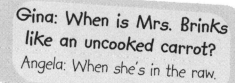

Angela: What do you get when you cross King with a tree?
Gordy: A dogwood.

Gordy: What do you get when you cross King with a cow?
Angela: A bulldog.

January: What do you get when you cross King with a moth?
Nanette: A mutt-erfly.

Bill: What do you get when you cross King and an elephant?
Gen: A greyhound.

Why did Angela Anaconda cross the road?
Because Nanette Manoir was on her side.

Why did Gordy Rhinehart cross the road?
To get to Gina Lash.

Why did Gina Lash
cross the road?
To get to Mapperson's Bakery.

Why did January Cole
cross the road?
To get to Nanette Manoir.

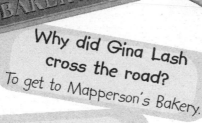

Le Salon

Why did Karlene Trainor
cross the road?
To get to Nanette Manoir even more.

January: Why did Gina Lash put a cinnamon bun on her head?

Karlene: She wanted to have naturally swirly hair.

Johnny: Is Gina's turtle still shy?
Gordy: No, he came out of his shell.

Gina: When Nanette's around, what's January and Karlene's favorite game?
Angela: Kiss the can.

Copycat Clone Club!

How did Gordy feel when Gina said hi to him?

It was the shy point of his day.

Why did Candy Mae think there'd be cookies at the square dance?
Because she'd heard there was going to be a lot of dough-si-dough.

38

Gordy: What's the best thing about riding in a garbage truck?
Angela: You get the pick of the litter.

Angela: What did you say when Mrs. Brinks found all your papers stuck together?
Johnny: "I didn't glue nothin'!"

Gordy: Why is Angela dancing with her dessert?
Gina: She wants to get jiggly with it.

44

What was Nanette doing in the boys' bathroom for so long?
Stalling.

Why did Gina head north for the winter?
She wanted to see A-LASH-ka.

Karlene: Why do Angela, Gina, Johnny, and Gordy always hang out with each other?

Nanette: Nerds of a feather flock together.

46

How is Nanette like Uncle Nicky's ceiling spitball?

They're both stuck-up.